THE LAST STAND

FIGHT THE CURE

HarperCollins®, ☰®, and HarperKidsEntertainment™
are trademarks of HarperCollins Publishers.

X-Men: The Last Stand: Fight the Cure
Marvel, X-Men and all related character names and the distinctive likenesses thereof
are trademarks of Marvel Characters, Inc., and are used with permission.
Copyright © 2006 Marvel Characters, Inc.
All rights reserved.
www.marvel.com
© 2006 Twentieth Century Fox Film Corporation.
Printed in the United States of America.
No part of this book may be used or reproduced in any manner whatsoever
without written permission except in the case of brief quotations embodied in critical articles and reviews.
For information address HarperCollins Children's Books, a division of HarperCollins Publishers,
1350 Avenue of the Americas, New York, NY 10019.
www.harperchildrens.com
Book design by John Sazaklis
Library of Congress catalog card number: 2006921078
ISBN-10: 0-06-082207-4 — ISBN-13: 978-0-06-082207-1
1 2 3 4 5 6 7 8 9 10
❖
First Edition

THE LAST STAND

FIGHT THE CURE

Adapted by Jasmine Jones

Based on the Motion Picture

written by Simon Kinberg & Zak Penn

 HarperKidsEntertainment

An Imprint of HarperCollinsPublishers

CHAPTER ONE

Wolverine took a deep breath and grinned. Overhead, a laser blast sliced through the air. There was a crash and a rumble, and a strong smell of smoke all around. A nearby building was on fire. *Perfect,* Wolverine thought. He always loved a good battle.

Rogue ran to him, her long dark hair flying. *Bang!*

An explosion tore through the air, sending pieces of metal flying at her!

Before Rogue had time to duck, a metal hand reached out and grabbed her arm. She looked up into the face of Colossus. Instantly, Rogue felt her body changing. . . .

Wolverine, Rogue, and Colossus weren't normal humans. They were X-Men—mutants with incredible powers. Wolverine could heal from any wound, and had metal claws under his skin. Colossus was strong, and his body could turn to metal. And Rogue could take on the power and memories of any person she touched.

Ping! Ping!

Bits of metal bounced off of Rogue's body. She had absorbed Colossus's power—for the moment, she was made of metal, too.

But Colossus didn't look well. Whenever Rogue used her talent, she drained the energy from the person whose power she took.

"You okay?" Rogue asked.

Colossus nodded weakly as an explosion shattered behind them.

Unconcerned, Wolverine pulled a piece of metal from his cheek. His face healed immediately.

"How long do we have?" Rogue asked. She sounded anxious.

"Two minutes . . ." Colossus glanced at Wolverine, waiting for a signal. "Tops."

"I'm away a few days and the whole world goes up in flames," Wolverine said. "You want to stand here and get shot?" Lifting an eyebrow, he glanced at a nearby door. It led to an underground bunker.

"If we hit that door," Rogue said, "we're clear."

Searchlights lit up the sky, revealing a tempest of laser blasts and machinery. This was an all-out war, and the X-Men were in the middle of it.

Nearby, Storm watched as Wolverine, Colossus, and Rogue darted toward the bunker. She was out of breath, tired from using her gift to fight the machines with lightning and fierce wind. Storm flew over to join the other two members of her

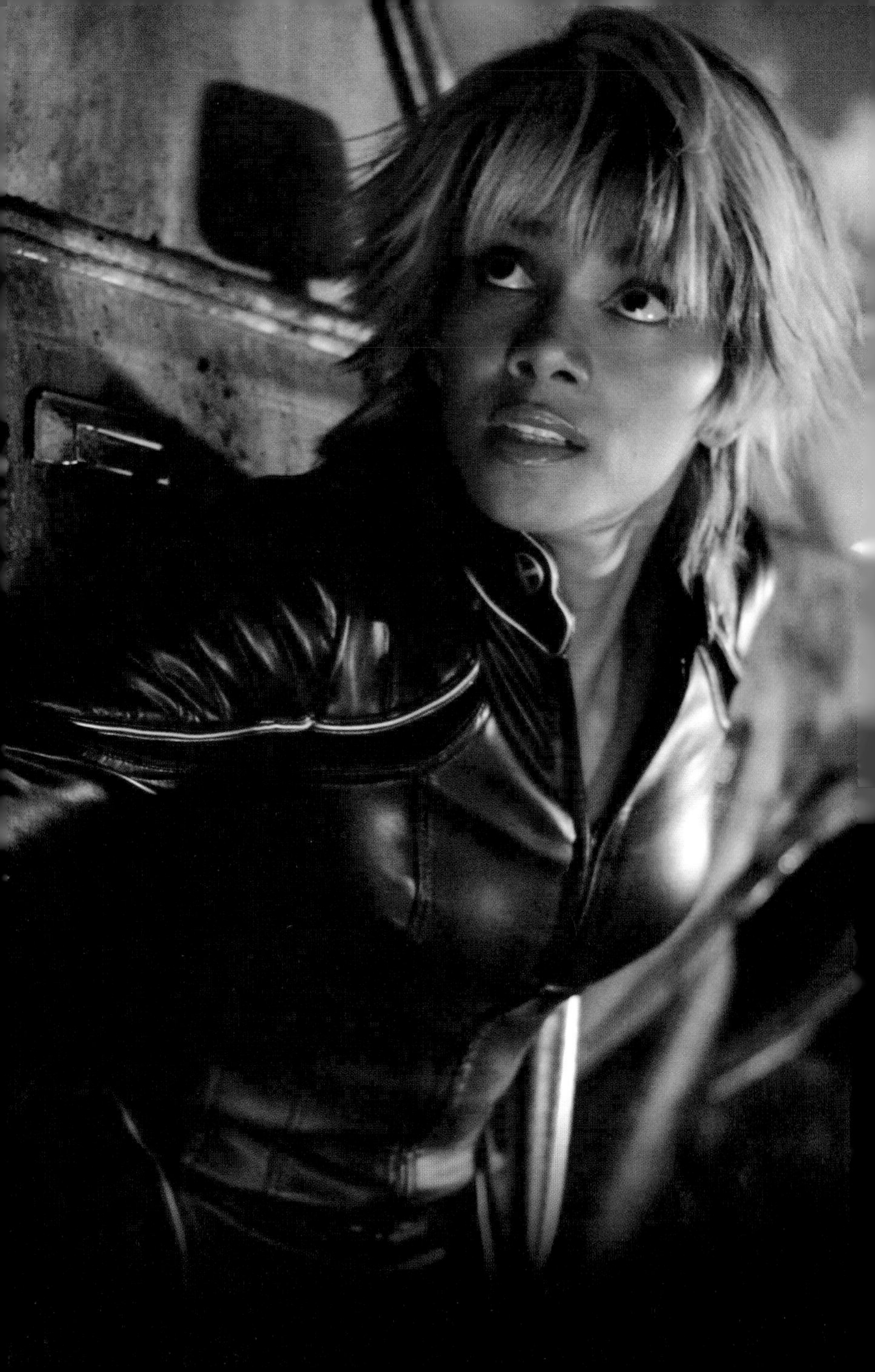

team—Kitty Pryde and Iceman.

A rocket whistled right at them, but before Storm could cry out, they phased together. This was Kitty's mutant power—she could become intangible so nothing would harm her. She could also pass through solid walls. The rocket passed by and exploded several yards away from them.

"You okay?" Kitty asked as she and Iceman separated.

"Yeah," Iceman said, catching his breath. "Only a quarter mile to the end."

"Right." Kitty nodded, her dark eyes flashing. "Follow my lead."

Iceman smiled. Kitty was new to the team, but he already knew that he liked her. A laser blast hurtled toward them, and Iceman unleashed a burst of ice. With a hiss, the blast turned to steam and harmlessly disappeared into the air.

When Iceman and Kitty caught up to Storm, she was staring down at a small electronic device on the sleeve of her uniform. It showed a map of the area. A counter in the corner ticked down. They only had one and a half minutes left.

"Let's pick it up," Storm said. She looked over at Wolverine, who was smiling.

He isn't taking this seriously, Storm thought in fury. *It's all a game to him!* Shaking off her rage, Storm plunged ahead. The other X-Men followed.

"Where is it?" Iceman asked, as the X-Men reached a dead end. "Can anybody see it?"

A shadow passed over them, casting the six mutants into darkness.

Wolverine looked up. Towering over them was an enormous robot—a Sentinel. It was more than a hundred feet high, and its gleaming steel dimly reflected the burning city. It paused only a moment to register the X-Men, then lunged at them.

Wolverine knew that they had to fight the machine if they wanted to win the battle. He suddenly had an idea. Colossus was strong. Very strong. If he could pick Wolverine up and throw him at the Sentinel, they might have a chance. As quickly as he could, Wolverine explained his idea to Colossus. "Throw me like a fastball!" he said.

In a flash, Colossus picked Wolverine up and hurled him at the enemy. As he flew through the air, Wolverine unleashed his metal claws and slashed at the Sentinel's neck upon impact.

The robot's metal head flew off and rolled to a stop at the feet of the stunned X-Men.

Suddenly, the smoldering cityscape disappeared around them. The X-Men were standing in a huge steel room. The entire battle had been a hologram—a virtual reality scene projected into the space around them. It was a training exercise to help the X-Men practice using their special talents. That was why the School for Gifted Youngsters existed—to teach and train the X-Men.

"I'm hungry," Wolverine growled. "Who wants pizza?" He turned to Colossus. "Hey, tin man, I've got to say, you throw like a girl . . . overhand."

Colossus nodded.

Storm shook her head as Wolverine

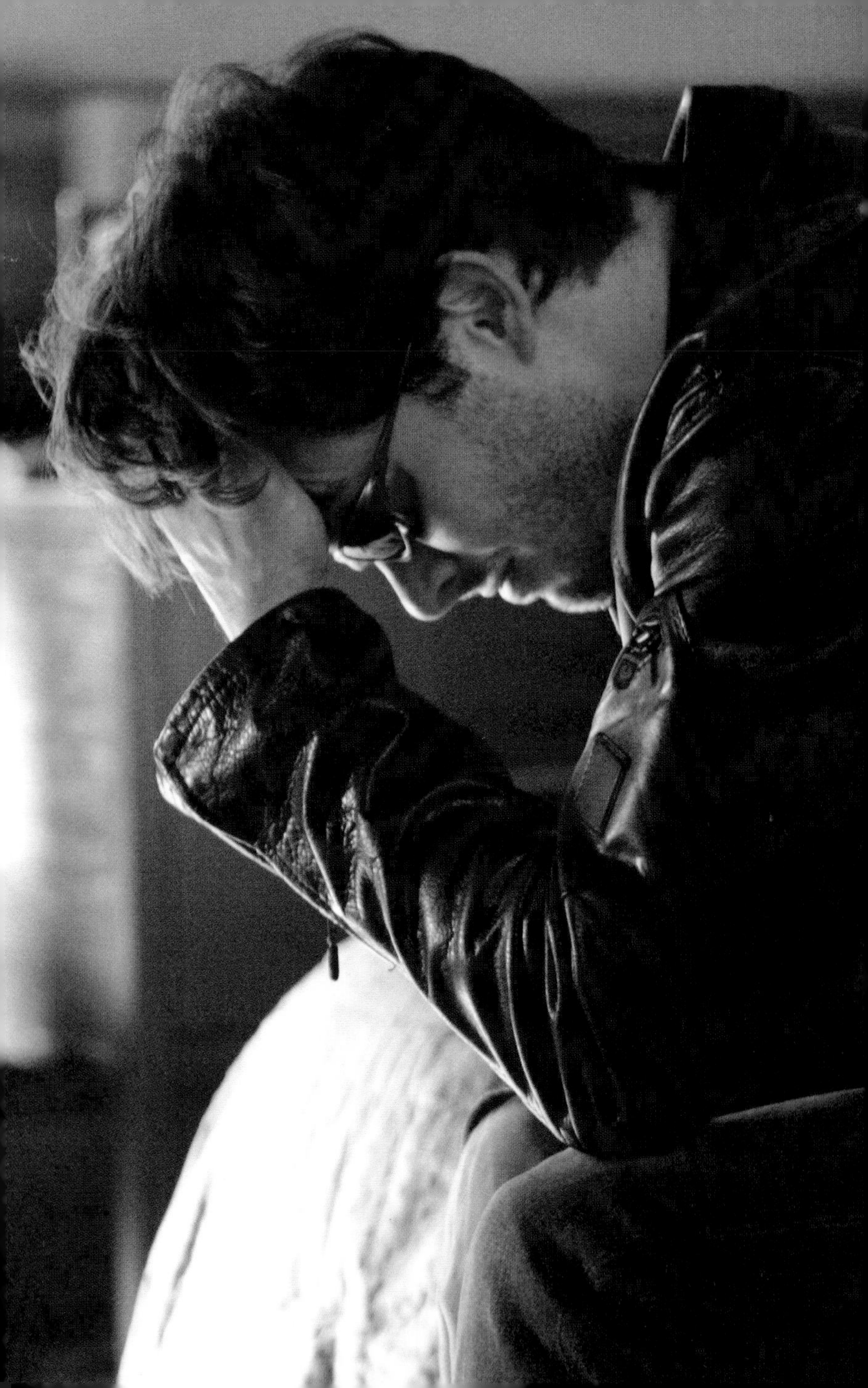

walked away. She hurried after him into the hallway.

"What was that?" Storm demanded.

"Danger Room session." Wolverine's voice was cool.

Storm narrowed her eyes. "You know what I mean. It was a defensive exercise."

"I'm just the sub," Wolverine said with a shrug. "If you've got a problem, then talk to Cyclops."

Cyclops could burn through metal with a single blast from his eyes, but he had been a wreck ever since Jean Grey died. Jean had been a talented and important member of the X-Men team. Everyone at the school was sad now that she was gone.

"No," Storm snapped. She was upset. "You can't just come and go as you please. We're trying to run a school here."

With a snarl, Wolverine stalked off. He wanted to have a word with Cyclops.

Wolverine finally found Cyclops in the garage. He was strapping a bag onto his silver Harley-Davidson motorcycle.

"We were looking for you downstairs," Wolverine said.

"What do you care?" Cyclops snapped. He stared at Wolverine from behind the ruby quartz visor that kept his laserbeam eyes from burning others.

"Well, I had to cover for you, for starters."

"I didn't ask you to," Cyclops pointed out.

"No," Wolverine said, "the professor did." He was talking about Professor Xavier, the founder of the school. "I know how you feel," Wolverine said, his usual growl softened.

Cyclops shook his head. "Don't—"

"When Jean died—" Wolverine began.

"DON'T!" Cyclops shouted.

Wolverine looked at him carefully for a moment. "Maybe it's time to move on."

Cyclops swallowed hard. "Not everyone heals as fast as you," he said, swinging himself onto the seat of his motorcycle. He revved the engine and rode away with a roar.

Wolverine watched him disappear. He could sense that Cyclops was going to look for Jean.

CHAPTER TWO

Professor Charles Xavier's wheelchair hummed quietly as he rolled up behind Storm, who was staring out of a window. The sky was dark and thunder rolled. Xavier knew what that meant—Storm was deeply troubled over something.

"I'm sorry," she said, turning to face him. Her cloudy eyes cleared, and the weather

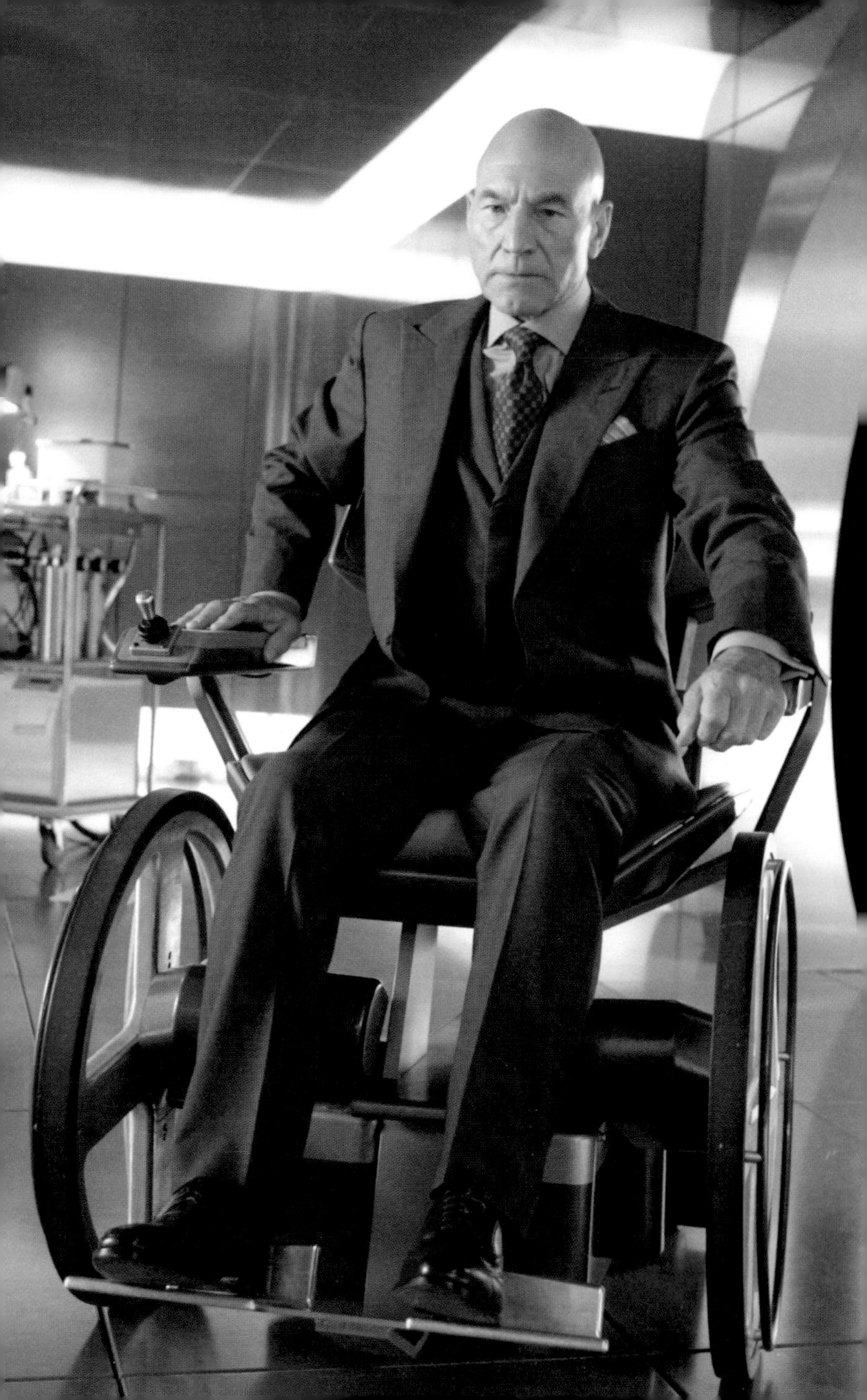

lifted instantly. Sighing, she looked out at the students, who were playing games using their mutant powers. It bothered Storm that the School for Gifted Youngsters was a secret from the outside world. "Magneto is a fugitive," she explained. "A mutant is in the executive branch of the government. We have a president who understands us. . . . Why are we still hiding?"

"We are *not* hiding," Xavier said. "I have to protect my students."

"We can't be students forever," Storm told him. She began walking down the hall, and the Professor rolled along beside her.

Xavier smiled softly. "I don't think of you as a student," he said. He spoke slowly, choosing his words carefully. "In fact, I can imagine you taking over for me one day."

Storm considered this for a moment. *Take over the school?* she thought. *I could never fill the professor's shoes!* "What about Cyclops?"

"He's taken Jean's death so hard," he said sadly. "And Logan's not interested." Logan was Wolverine's real name.

They stopped in front of the professor's office, where a large blue furry mutant in a business suit stood waiting. This was Beast. He worked with the president of the United States as secretary of mutant affairs.

Beast did not look happy. He explained that the government had caught Mystique, the metamorph. He was worried this might make

Magneto come out of hiding. But there was more. "A major pharmaceutical company has developed a mutant antibody," he explained. "A way to suppress the mutant gene . . . permanently." The government had found a way to "cure" mutants—to make them normal.

Storm gaped at Beast. "Since when is being a mutant a disease?"

✳✳✳✳✳✳

A few days later, the students at the School for Gifted Youngsters were gathered around a television set, listening to Warren Worthington Sr. Few people knew that his son, Warren Worthington Jr., was a mutant.

Ever since Warren Worthington Sr. discovered the white-feathered wings growing from his son's back, he devoted his own company

to finding a cure. "They've been labeled saints and sinners—monsters," Mr. Worthington said. "But they are people just like us. Their affliction is nothing more than a disease. Finally, there is hope. There is now a cure!" He explained that Alcatraz—the island in San Francisco Bay that had formerly been used as a prison—was where his company would begin to administer the cure.

"There's nothing to cure," Storm said. Her voice was cold as steel. "Who would want this cure? What kind of coward would take it just to fit in?"

Beast walked into the room, frowning at Storm. "Not all of us have such an easy time fitting in," he pointed out. "You don't shed on the furniture."

"Enough," Xavier said.

Just then, Rogue rushed into the room. "Is it true?" she asked in a breathless voice. "They can cure us?"

"No, because there's nothing to cure," Storm shot back. "There's nothing wrong with you."

Rogue swallowed hard. Her "gift" was a difficult one. She hurt anyone she touched. She knew she was supposed to be grateful for her talent . . . but it wasn't always easy.

Storm shook her head. She had spent a lifetime trying to feel normal. But this cure made her feel like an outcast again.

CHAPTER THREE

When Wolverine heard Professor Xavier cry out, he ran to his office to find out what had happened. Storm was already there.

"You must go to Alkalai Lake," the professor insisted. His face was pale. "Now!"

Wolverine and Storm hurried to the *X-Jet*. Storm took the controls and guided the plane to the last place that anyone had seen Jean Grey. Wolverine stared out the window.

When they landed at the lake, it was clear that something had happened. Cyclops's visor was sitting on the beach. Water rippled up the veins of a leaf. A rock balanced strangely on its edge.

Looking down, Storm caught sight of Jean, who appeared to collapse. "She's alive!" Storm cried.

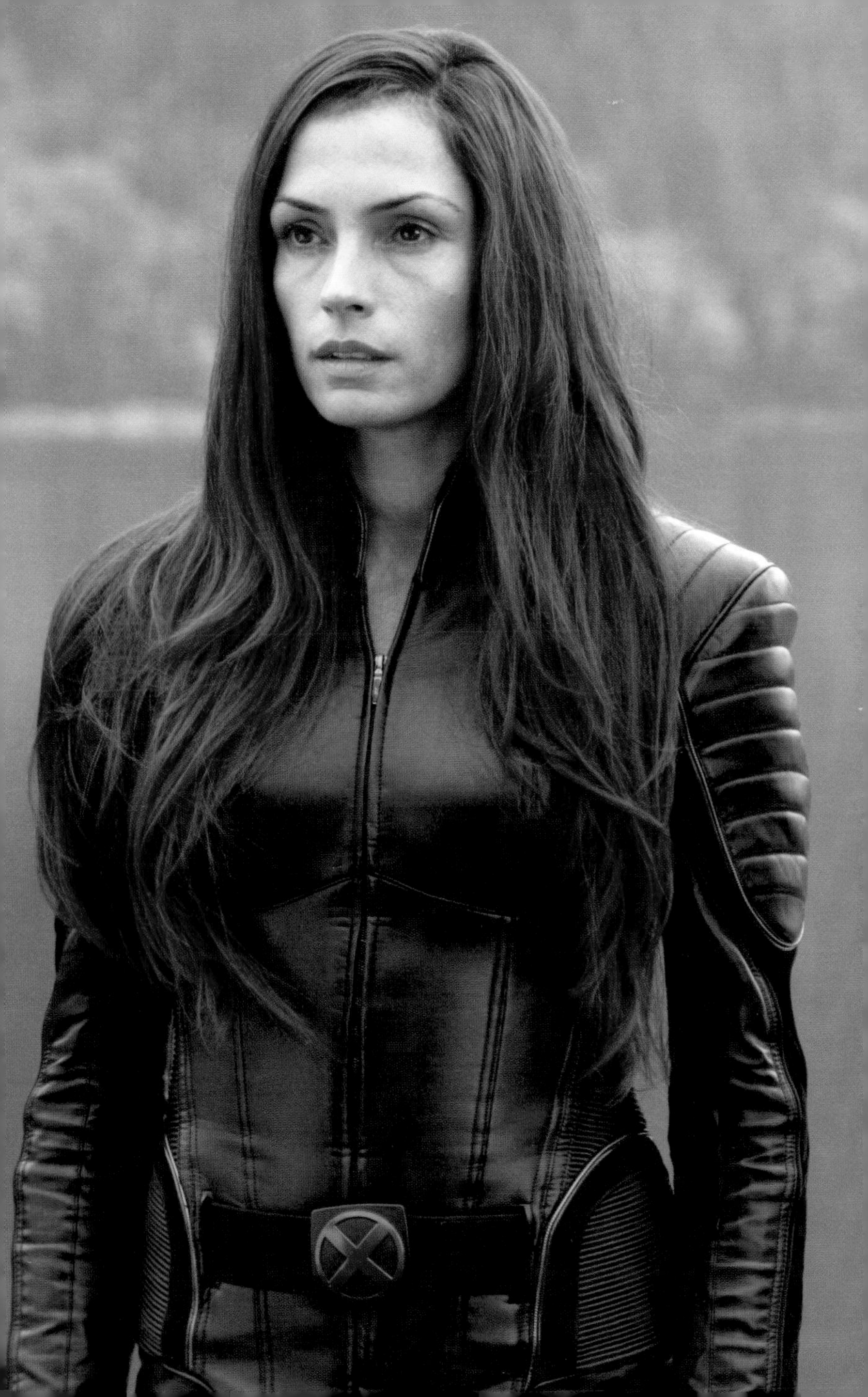

As quickly and carefully as they could, Storm and Wolverine carried Jean to the *X-Jet* and then flew her to the school. The doctors—and the professor—would take care of her there.

"Where am I?" Jean asked when she woke up. Her voice was scratchy, her vision blurry.

Wolverine looked at her carefully. Professor Xavier had explained that Jean had a dark

side—one even she didn't know about. Sometimes she was Jean Grey. And sometimes she was the Phoenix. Many years ago, Xavier had decided to protect Jean from herself, so he used his powers to help lock away the Phoenix. But now Xavier was worried that the Phoenix was back. And Wolverine was starting to worry, too. "What happened to Cyclops?" Wolverine asked.

Jean began to tremble. Suddenly, she

remembered. Cyclops had come to the lake to find her. But she had been the Phoenix then—her powers had been out of control. She had killed him by mistake. "Oh, no," she said, tears flowing down her face. Objects began to float around the room, and Jean's voice sounded strange.

"The professor can help you," Wolverine said. "He can fix you."

"I don't want to be fixed," Jean said loudly, rising abruptly from the hospital bed. But she wasn't Jean anymore. She was the Phoenix. "I'm *free* now." She blasted Wolverine into the wall of the infirmary with her strong powers of levitation. He fell to the floor, unconscious.

The Phoenix raised her hand, and the door opened. She walked through, and did not look back.

"When will he learn?" Xavier asked as he wheeled himself down the hall with Storm. "We'll never get what we want by force." They had just heard that Magneto was back. He had attacked a truck convoy and freed several mutants, including Juggernaut and Multiple Man. But he was too late for Mystique. Before she could escape, a guard had shot her with the mutant cure. She was now a human.

Professor Xavier stopped short as he and Storm arrived at the infirmary. It was a disaster zone.

Wolverine stumbled in behind them. He explained that Jean had attacked him. "She's not herself," he said. "I think . . . she killed Cyclops." He was distraught.

Storm's eyes grew wide in shock, but the professor wasn't surprised. "I warned you about this," he said. Using his thoughts, Xavier tried to find Jean. They had to stop her.

But the Phoenix was too strong—she blocked his thoughts.

Xavier had an idea. He thought he might know where Jean was going. "I hope we are not too late," he said.

"Wait outside," Xavier said to Wolverine and Storm as they pulled up in front of Jean Grey's childhood home. It was here that, years earlier, Xavier had first met Jean Grey when she was just thirteen years old. Magneto had been there, too.

And Magneto was there now. He had arrived with two of his followers—Callisto and Juggernaut. Callisto had sensed Jean's presence, and had warned him that, as the Phoenix, she was more powerful than any other mutant.

Magneto gave Xavier a cruel smile. "You were right, Charles," he said, his eyes gleaming evilly. "This one is special."

Wolverine watched anxiously as Xavier went inside with Magneto to talk to Jean. Wolverine didn't know which side the Phoenix would choose to be on.

Around him, objects began to levitate. There was a crash inside the house. Then a mailbox shuddered. Wolverine started toward the house, but Storm held him back.

"Xavier told us to wait here," Storm said. "He said he'd handle this."

Wolverine's nostrils flared angrily, but he stayed put. He eyed Juggernaut. If anything happened to Xavier, Wolverine was ready to take on Magneto and his henchmen.

Inside the house, Magneto and Xavier were battling for Jean.

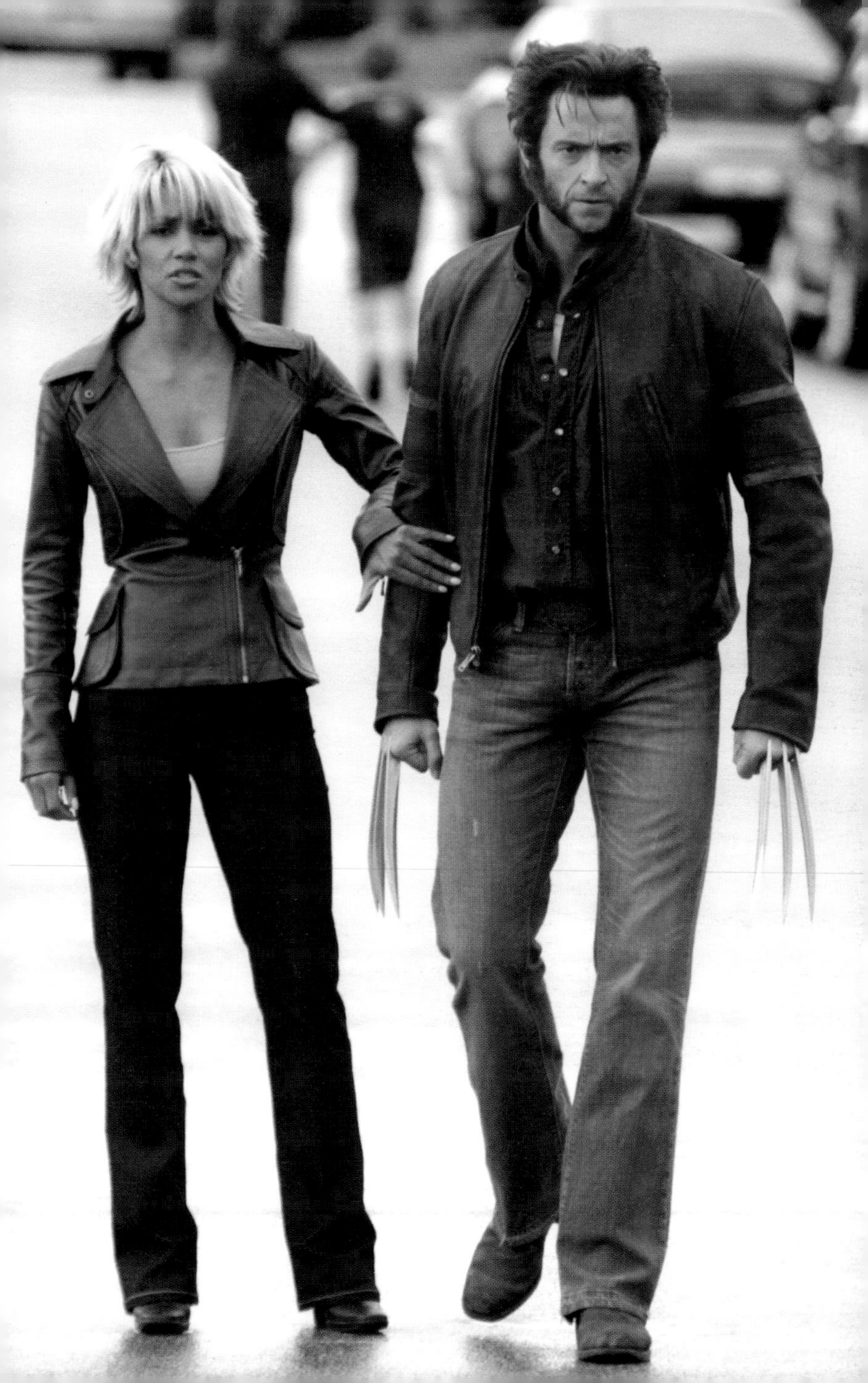

"Look at me, Jean!" Xavier said. His lips didn't move, though. He could communicate directly with Jean's mind.

"No!" Jean shot back. "Stay out of my head." She began to glow with an eerie light— the Phoenix was again rising within her.

"Yes," Magneto hissed. "It's time for you to be free."

"Jean, I won't ask again," Xavier told her.

"Get out, both of you!" Jean cried mentally.

A lamp flew through the room and crashed against a wall. Bookshelves were emptied. A table rose into the air. Jean was so upset that her emotions were making things move. Gravity began to reverse. Xavier's wheelchair rose into the air; then he was elevated out of it. It looked as though he were standing a few feet off the ground.

Outside the house, Wolverine lashed out at Juggernaut. Callisto ran to help, but Storm stopped her with a blast of lightning.

Juggernaut lowered his head and crashed into Wolverine. Together, they broke through a wall.

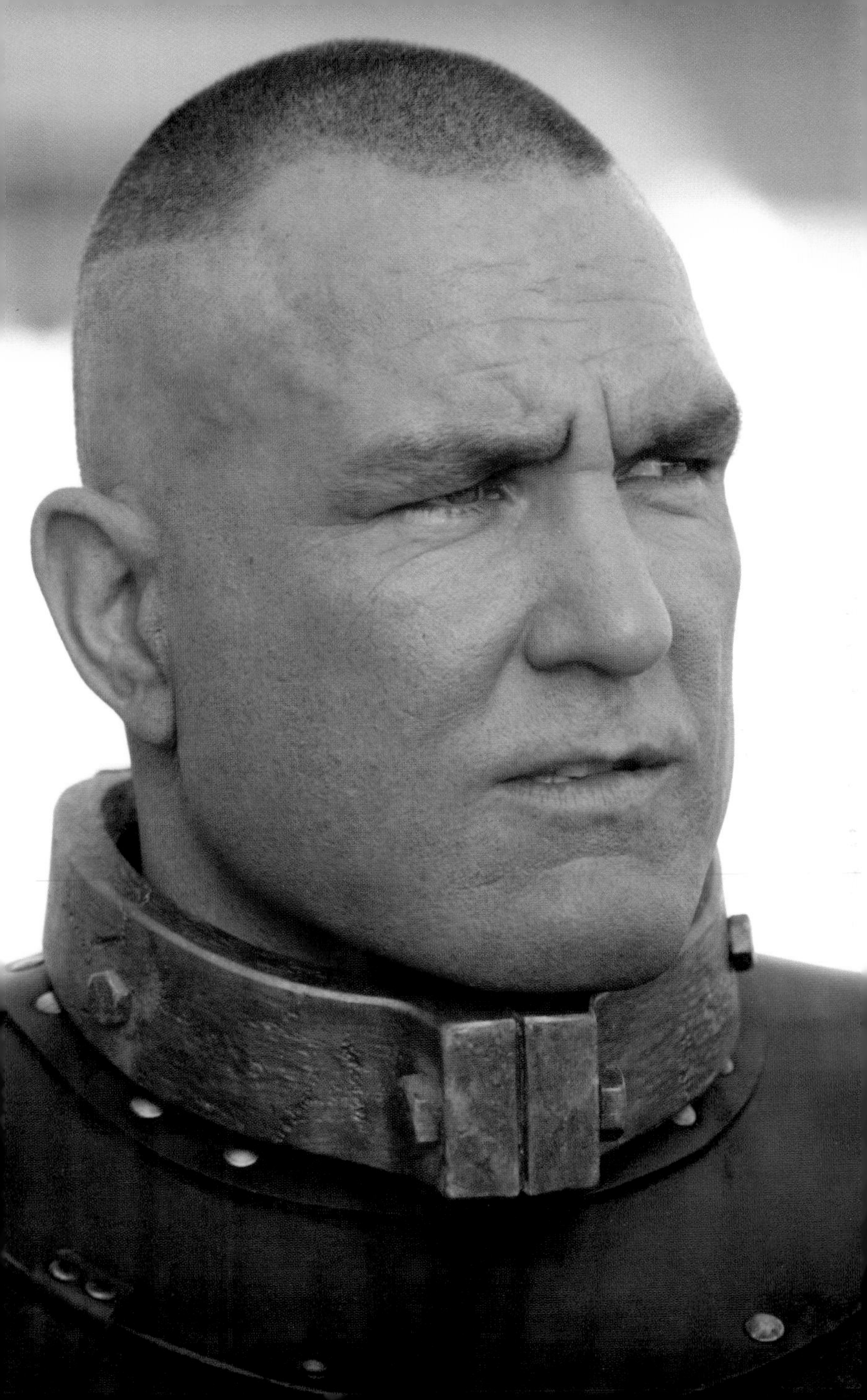

Back inside, the objects in the room were beginning to dissolve. Suddenly, Professor Xavier's body began to disappear. Xavier looked at Jean. He knew that she couldn't help what she was doing. But he was disintegrating, atom by atom. "Don't let it control you," Xavier whispered into her mind.

A moment later, there was a burst of light.

Magneto stood there, staring at the place where Xavier had been only a moment before. Finally, he turned to Jean. "Do you know what you've done?" he said. "Freed me and yourself. Join me, and you will be free from this day forward."

Jean followed him out of the house without a word.

At the sight of Jean with Magneto, every hair on Wolverine's body stood on end. For the moment, the fight with Callisto and Juggernaut was completely forgotten. He and Storm raced inside the house.

"*No!*" Wolverine cried when he saw Xavier's empty wheelchair.

But it was too late. The professor was gone.

CHAPTER FOUR

Storm stood over two empty graves. X-Men from all over the world had gathered to pay their respects to Cyclops and Xavier.

"We live in an age of darkness," Storm said, as she looked out at the sorrowful faces around her. "But in every age, there are those who fight against it. Charles Xavier was born into a world divided, a world he tried to heal. Wherever we may go, we must carry

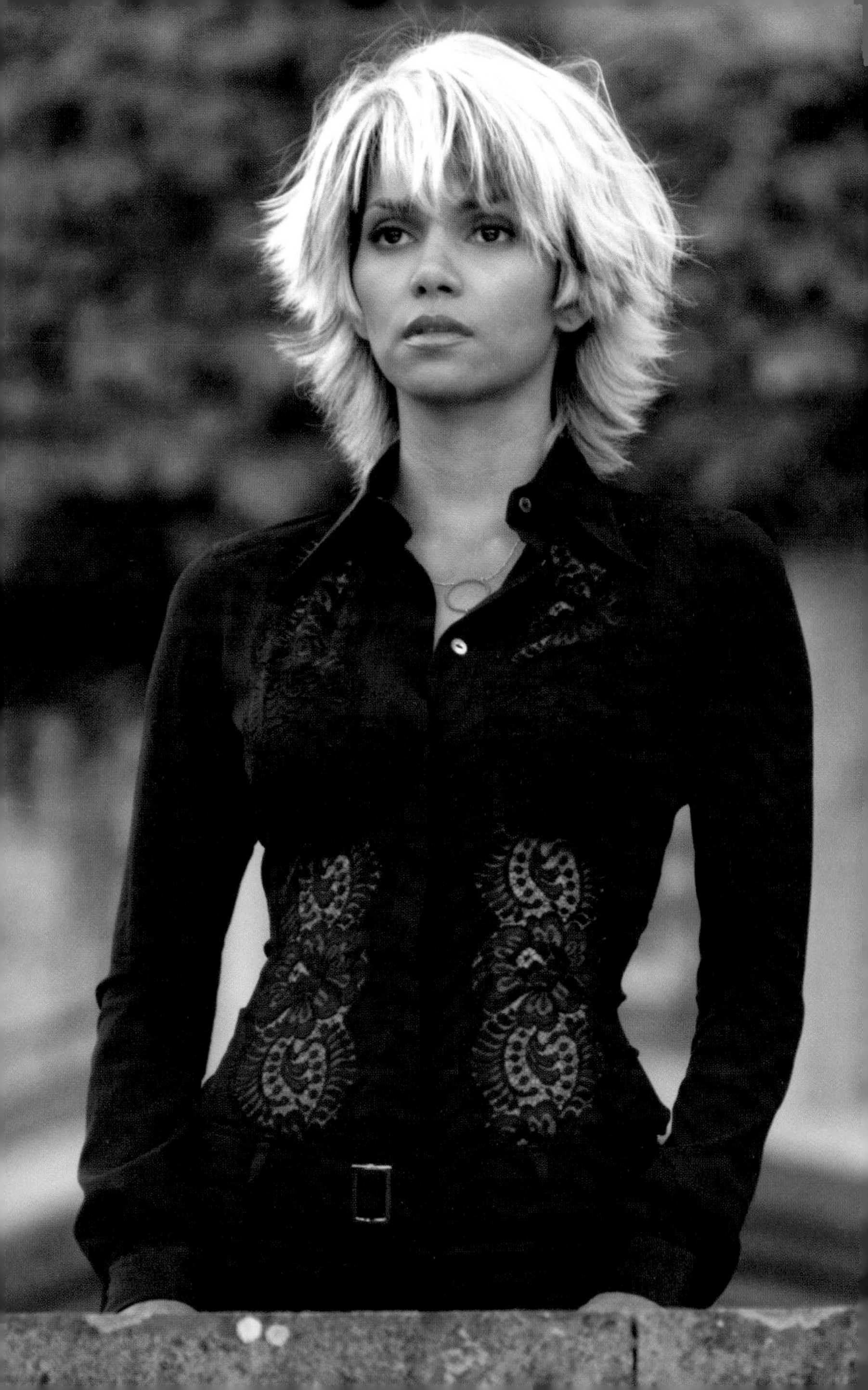

on his vision—the vision of a world united."

A tear trickled down Rogue's face. Storm noticed that almost everyone associated with the School for Gifted Youngsters was there—Colossus, Kitty, Iceman, Xavier's old friend Moira MacTaggert . . . even Beast had come up from Washington, D.C. Only one X-Man was absent.

Wolverine was nowhere to be seen.

Later that day, Storm confronted Wolverine. She knew that he wanted to go look for Jean. But Storm didn't want to lose any more friends to the Phoenix's dark power.

"Why can't you let her go?" Storm asked. "Why can't you see the truth?"

Wolverine glared at her, his lips curled into a snarl.

"Because you love her," Storm went on, her voice gentle. "She made her choice. It's time to make yours. If you're with us, then be sure you're *with* us." Storm's dark, liquid eyes filled with tears, and her voice was husky as she went on. "I've lost two of my oldest friends and the only father I've ever known. I don't want to lose you, too."

Wolverine's face, which had hardened into an angry mask, began to soften. He watched Storm as she walked away, but he did not speak.

Storm had left him to make his choice—stay with the X-Men or find Jean. Now all he had to do was decide.

Worried, Storm pressed her lips together as students and teachers talked about closing the School for Gifted Youngsters. Her heart thudded in her chest. *Without Charles Xavier or Cyclops, who would run the school?* She knew she couldn't do it alone. She wasn't ready yet.

On the other hand, the thought of closing the school made her heart ache. Not only was it a beautiful building with state-of-the-art teaching equipment, it was also the only place where mutant children could feel safe.

Storm remembered how lonely she had been before she found the school. With her long white hair and dark skin, she had stood out as a child even before she had discovered her mutant ability. But once Storm had realized that she could control the weather, the other children in her neighborhood avoided her completely.

It was only when Charles Xavier brought her to the school that Storm was able to feel normal. And she knew that Rogue, Iceman, Colossus, Kitty, and the other X-Men felt the same way.

It was at that very moment that an angel appeared.

A young man staggered into the school in a trenchcoat, huge white wings trailing behind him. He was bedraggled and his eyes were huge with fright as he stared at the room full of X-Men.

"I know this is a bad time," the boy with the white wings said, "but my name is Warren Worthington."

A murmur rippled through the room. Storm sucked in her breath. Warren Worthington? That was the name of the man who had

created the so-called cure for mutants. *This must be his son!* Storm realized.

Warren looked around the room. "I was told this was a safe place for mutants."

"It was . . ." Beast said.

"No." Storm took a step forward. She knew at that moment that she had to take over the school. This boy had come here seeking help, and he was going to get it. Storm looked out at the roomful of questioning faces. It was time to take a stand. "It *is*."

She turned to Iceman and said, "Show Mr. Worthington to a room and tell all the students the school will remain open."

Wolverine looked down at Xavier's grave. He regretted missing the funeral. But he just couldn't go. It was too painful.

His fingers trailed over the headstone. Suddenly, an image floated into Wolverine's mind. Or was it a voice . . . ? It was Jean. "Come to me," she whispered. "Help me."

An image blasted into Wolverine's mind. With a shock, he realized that he was seeing an entire scene—Jean was sending him a vision of where she was. The woods. Darkness. There were mutants, many of them. Among the crowd, there was one face in particular that Wolverine recognized.

Magneto.

Then Wolverine saw himself at the campsite. Jean was there. But there were too many mutants guarding the path. He couldn't get to her. He fought, slashing his way through the outer guard, but Magneto's Brotherhood of Mutants was too strong. . . .

Wolverine's eyes clicked open. He was back in the present, at the gravesite. But Wolverine was a hunter. He could track anything, human or beast. And Jean had sent him a clear message. He could still hear her voice in his mind. "Help me," she said.

That was enough. Wolverine was going to look for Jean.

Wolverine roared up to the mutant campsite on his motorcycle. At first, his plan was simple: take on the Brotherhood, tear through them, and rescue Jean.

But when Wolverine looked down at the campsite, he realized that he wasn't simply up against a small band of rebel mutants.

He was up against an army.

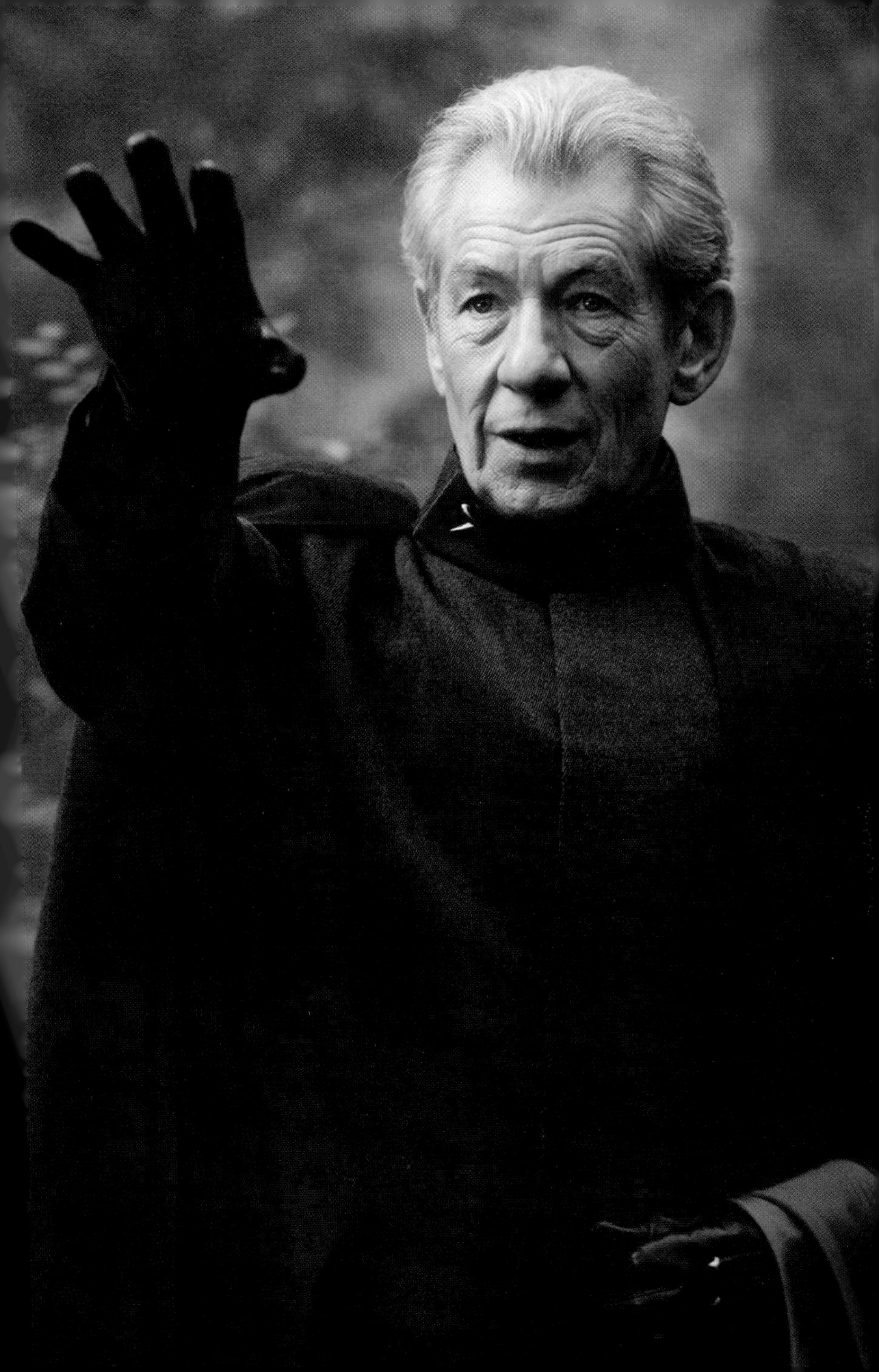

Hundreds of mutants had joined Magneto in the battle against the mutant cure. There was no way that Wolverine could take on so many at once.

After hesitating for a few moments, Wolverine crept through the woods, blending in to the crowd. Magneto was at the center, giving a speech. Wolverine caught his breath when he saw who was beside him—it was Jean. But she was glowing strangely. She was the Phoenix.

"They say we're criminals," Magneto shouted to the large crowd of mutants. "They wish to *cure* us."

The crowd of mutants booed. A sneer crept up the side of Magneto's face. "They have their weapons." He looked over at Jean. "We have ours."

The mutants quieted as they stared at the Phoenix. They knew that she was more powerful than any of them—possibly more powerful than all of them put together—and they were afraid. But they were also proud to have her join the battle.

Wolverine moved toward her as stealthily

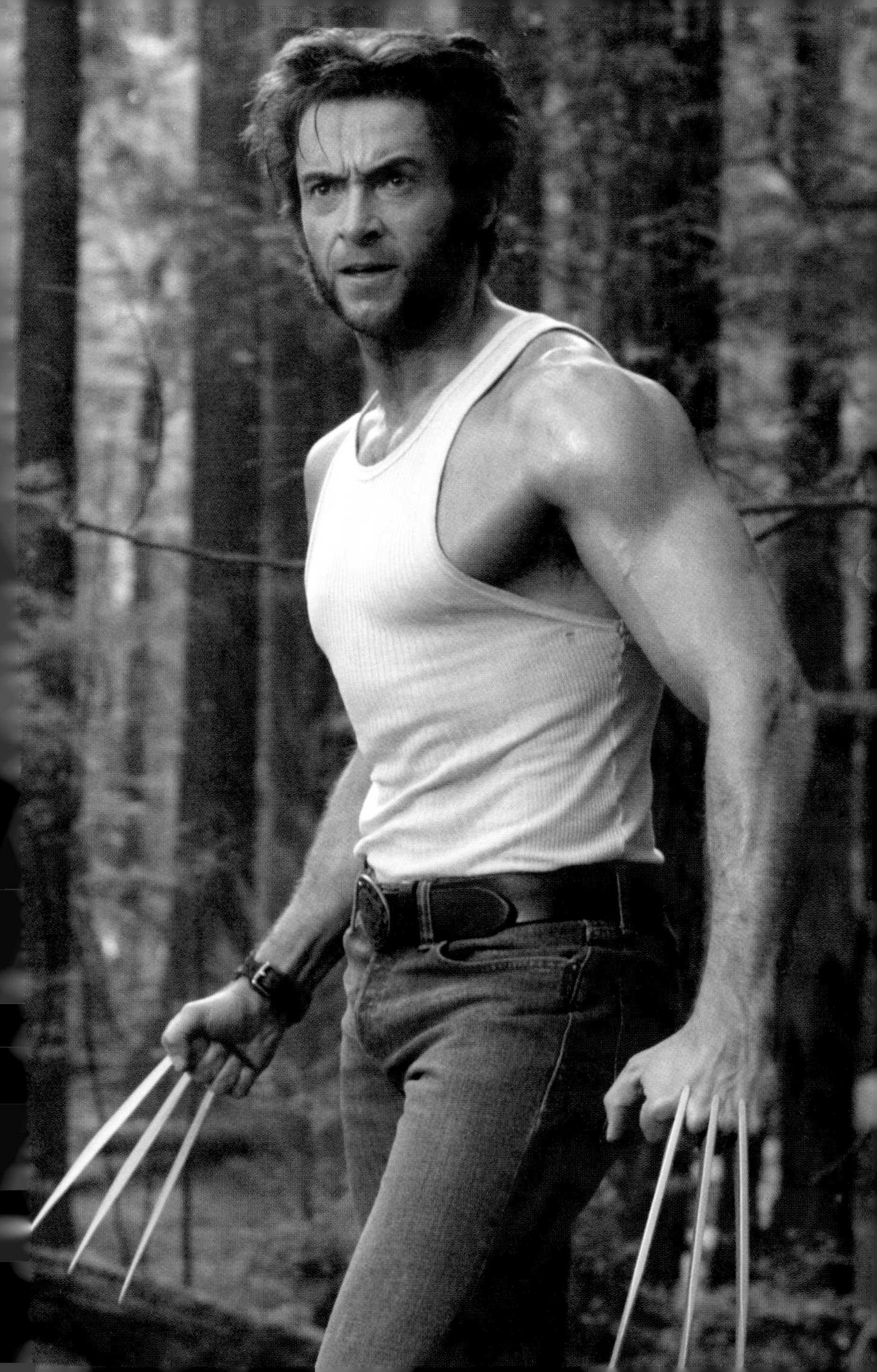

as he could. When Jean saw him, her glow faltered and her eyes cleared.

She knows me, Wolverine realized. He knew that for the moment at least, Jean was back to herself.

But Magneto had also caught Jean's look. He glanced over at Wolverine. "I do admire your persistence," he said calmly.

"You think you're gonna scare me off?" Wolverine asked.

Magneto put a hand on Wolverine's chest. The metal skeleton in Wolverine's body responded to Magneto's powers as, with a shove, Magneto launched Wolverine through the forest. With a sickening thud, Wolverine slammed into a tree.

He lay there, bleeding, trying to catch his breath.

I can't take on Magneto alone, Wolverine realized. Jean is confused. Half of her is the Phoenix and wants to stay with Magneto. The other half wants to come with me. But I can't save her all by myself.

I need help.

Back at the school, Wolverine made his way into the hangar and headed toward the *X-Jet*.

A group of X-Men stood waiting for him. Wolverine hesitated a moment, eyeing Iceman, Kitty, Colossus, Warren Worthington Jr.—now known as Angel—Storm, and Beast.

Wolverine waited for the others to board the jet. Just as he was about to join them, Rogue appeared in the hangar and hurried over to him.

"You almost missed the flight," Wolverine said, gesturing to the *X-Jet*. "Let's go."

Rogue shook her head and reached out to touch his arm. "I'm not going."

Wolverine looked down at Rogue's hand. She wasn't wearing her protective gloves. Her bare skin was touching his—but she wasn't draining his life force.

She is cured.

Wolverine's eyes met Rogue's.

"You don't know what it's like to be afraid of your powers—afraid to get close to anyone, to know you can never go home again," she said,

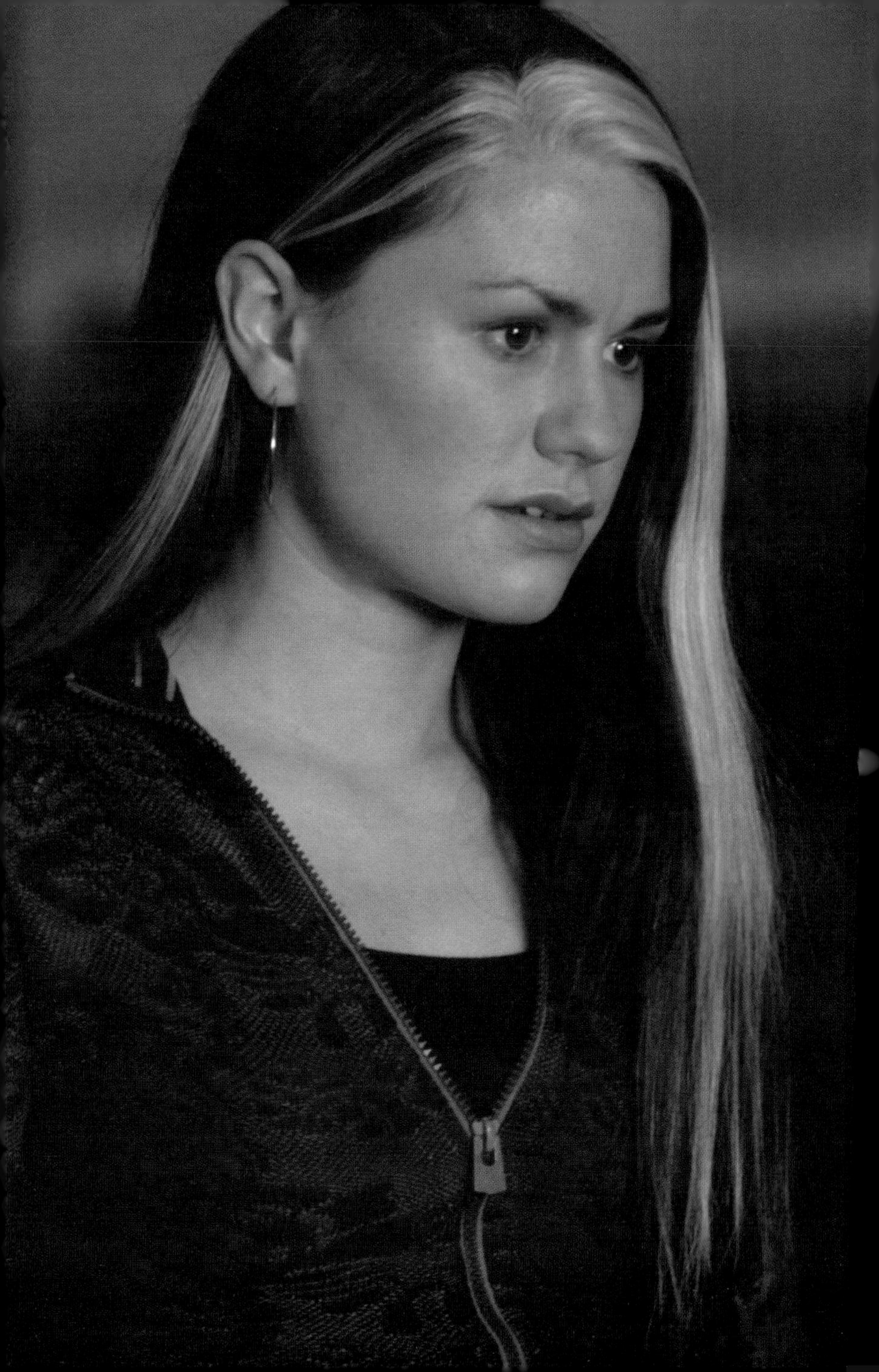

her eyes filling with tears.

Wolverine thought about the power he had never asked for. Wolverine didn't even know where he was from or how old he was. And he thought about Jean—how strong her powers were, and how divided against herself she was. "I do," he told Rogue, "and I'm not going to judge you."

"Be careful," Rogue said.

With a nod, Wolverine boarded the jet.

"You know we're going there to stop Magneto," Storm said as she piloted the plane to Alcatraz. They knew that Magneto was going to go after the source of the cure—to destroy it. "If Jean's there . . ." Storm said, "if she's with him . . ."

"Storm, if she *is* there, I want you to get everyone away from her," Wolverine said.

"What are you going to do?" Storm asked.

"I know what she's capable of," Wolverine told her. He looked out of the window of the *X-Jet*. "If I have to . . . I'll choose the lesser evil."

Storm shivered. This was going to be a terrible battle, and she was afraid . . . for all of them.

CHAPTER FIVE

The Golden Gate Bridge had begun to shake. The metal cables that supported the bridge began to buckle and then pull apart. On the bridge, cars screeched to avoid falling over the edge.

Magneto was ripping it to shreds.

Part of the bridge almost collided with the *X-Jet* as it prepared to land. With a swift move, Storm dodged the faltering bridge.

The battle was about to begin. Magneto's army was already marching on Alcatraz, determined to locate the cure. In fact, Callisto had already used her powers to determine the source of the cure—a mutant named Leech. He had the power to turn mutants human. Anything from his body could do this—a strand of hair or a piece of his fingernail.

Jean watched from the bridge as the *X-Jet* landed on the island. She had been following Magneto, but stopped when she saw humans suffering. Now she was at war with herself. The Phoenix longed to plunge into battle—to unleash her power and destroy the cure. But Jean knew that Magneto was wrong. Violence was never the answer. And so she stood on the Golden Gate Bridge, unable to move, as the two armies prepared to do battle on Alcatraz Island.

The X-Men gathered around the Worthington Labs Compound. Soldiers assembling to defend the cure held up their weapons. They had heard that a mutant army was coming for the cure—and they thought that the X-Men were part of that army. Warren Worthington Sr. was with them. He didn't want anything to happen to his cure.

Just then, Warren Worthington Jr.—Angel—stepped out of the *X-Jet*.

"Hold on," Angel cried. "Let me explain."

"Wait," Mr. Worthington called. "Don't fire."

He looked at his son, then took in the X-Men. "What are you doing here?"

"*Helping* you," Beast replied.

"Magneto is going after the source of the cure," Storm explained. "Where is it?"

Mr. Worthington hesitated.

"Dad, please," Angel begged.

"On the second floor," Mr. Worthington said finally. "Southeast corner."

Wolverine looked at the other X-Men. "Let's move out."

At that moment, Magneto attacked.

"Take cover!" Wolverine cried as a stack of burning cars flew from the bridge toward the island. He and the rest of the X-Men hurried down into the fight.

Thunder rolled as Storm blasted Magneto's mutants from the air. Wolverine fought like an animal, taking on several mutants at a time. Angel flew overhead, picking up mutants and dropping them—until Magneto hurled a hunk of metal into the sky, clipping his wing. Angel plunged to the ground. Pyro bore down on him, but Iceman saw him coming. He blasted

a shot of ice at the fiery mutant. Pyro fought back with a burst of flame, but Iceman blocked his shot with a freezing wall.

Callisto found Storm. Soon, they were locked in battle again, just as they had been in front of Jean Grey's house. Callisto could move at incredible speeds. Storm tried to blast her, but she dodged away too quickly.

Nearby, Magneto had set his sights on the main building of the Worthington compound.

He was hovering overhead, hitting the structure with all the power he had, ripping apart the steel beams that held the building together and blasting it with huge chunks of metal.

Wolverine stared in horror. In moments, nothing would be left. Quickly, Wolverine turned to Colossus. "Hey, tin man," Wolverine said. "How 'bout that move again?"

Colossus shook his head at him, confused.

"You know," Wolverine prompted. "The fastball special?"

With a quick nod, Colossus heaved Wolverine off of his feet. And in a flash, he hurled him through the air.

Slam!

"Where is she?" Wolverine cried as he blasted into Magneto. "Where is Jean?"

Magneto whirled and fought back, but the air around him began to swirl. Suddenly, a blast of lightning struck him. Storm was helping Wolverine.

But Magneto was too strong. He slammed Storm with a hunk of metal, then held out his hand, freezing Wolverine in midair.

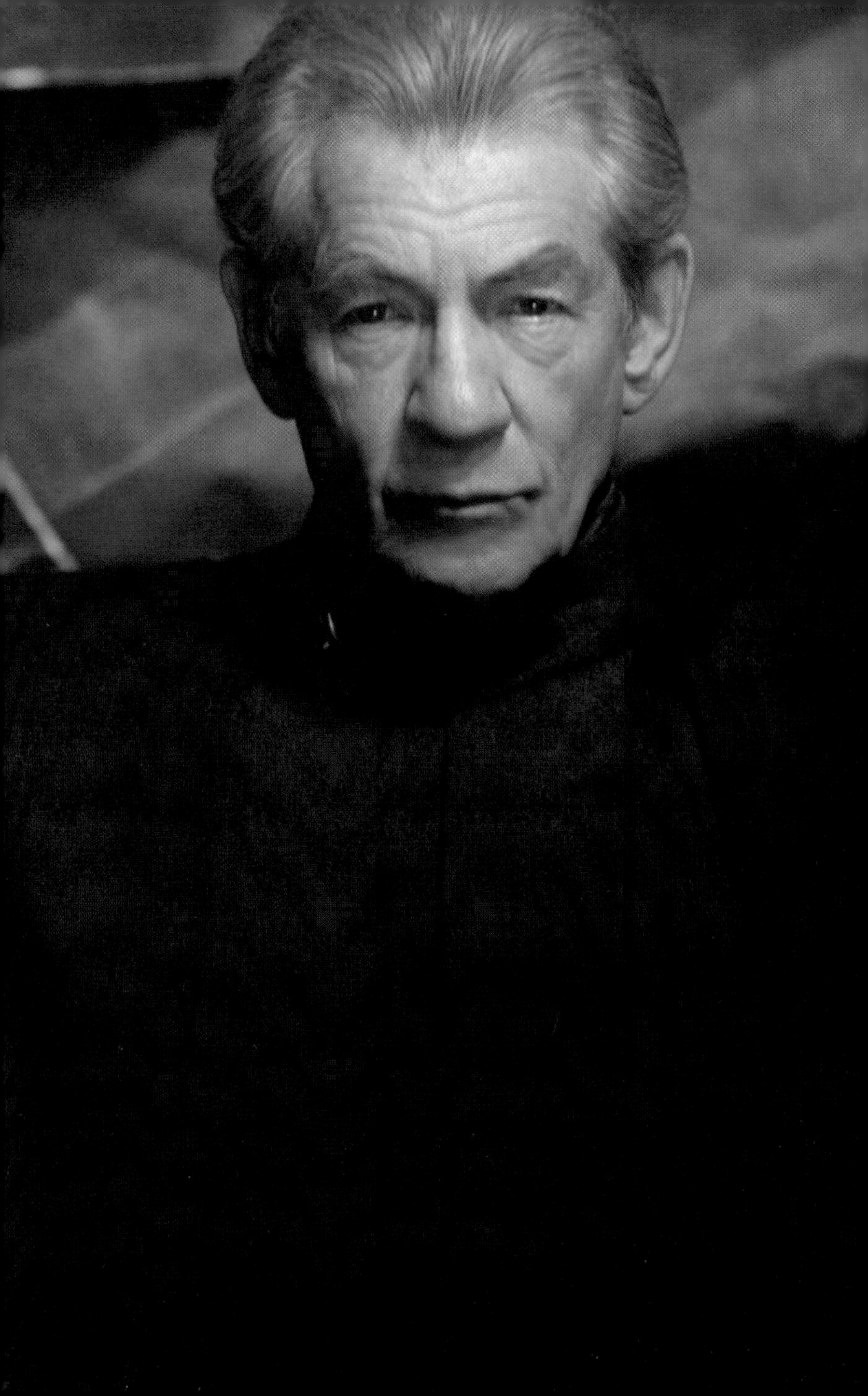

"When *will* you learn your lesson?" Magneto asked.

Just then, Magneto felt himself being shoved backward. He crashed through a wall as Jean stepped in to rescue Wolverine.

Wolverine dropped to the ground, then stood and faced Jean. *I can save her,* he thought.

At that very moment, a group of soldiers shot at Jean. The bullets knocked her backward. When she stood up, there was a new fire in her eyes. . . . The Phoenix had risen.

She attacked with full force.

Energy spiraled in all directions, flattening buildings, making the night in San Francisco as bright as day. Flames curled like wings around the Phoenix as her energy began to rip the island to shreds.

"Get everybody off the island!" Wolverine called. X-Men and humans alike began to flee Jean's deadly power.

Wolverine started after Jean.

"No!" Storm shouted.

"This is one thing I have to do alone," Wolverine told her. "I'm the only person who

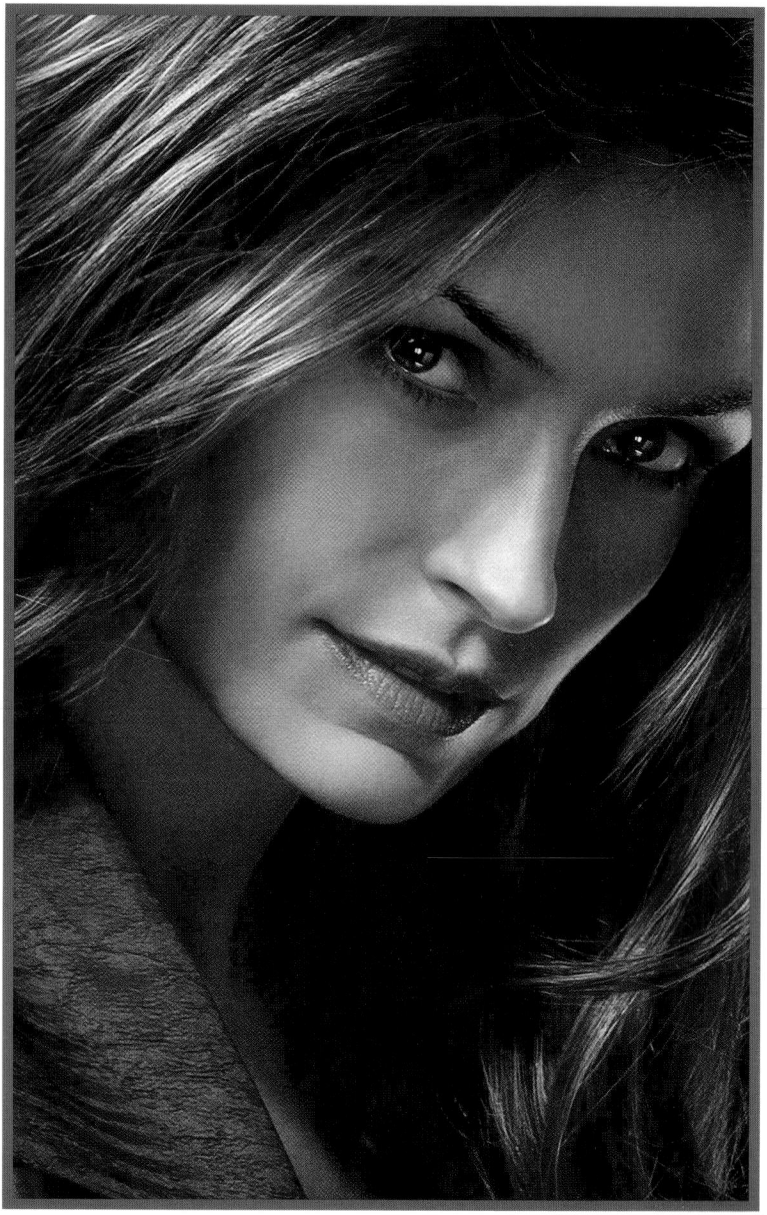

can get close enough to Jean to stop her."

Jean's power tore across the island, destroying the buildings and the cure supplies inside. Wolverine walked toward her. As he got closer, his skin began to dissolve, just as Xavier's had. But Wolverine had the power to heal. As quickly as his body disappeared, it reappeared again. He screamed in pain, but he did not stop, did not turn back. He wouldn't leave until he had helped Jean.

Wolverine stared deeply into Jean's eyes. Then he lifted his hand, claws out.

"Save me," Jean whispered.

Wolverine nodded.

With a quick stroke, he drove his claws through the Phoenix. The fire in her eyes went out. The glow around her disappeared. For an instant, she was Jean again. She looked up at Wolverine and smiled.

A moment later, she died.

Tears flowed from Wolverine's eyes as he gathered Jean's body in his arms and carried her off the island. The battle was over.

But it had cost the X-Men dearly.

CHAPTER SIX

Back at the School for Gifted Youngsters, Storm was setting up her office. She had taken over as head of the school, and a new semester was about to begin.

"I thought I might teach history," Beast explained, "and third-period Latin."

Storm and Beast walked out the front doors and were confronted with a long line of

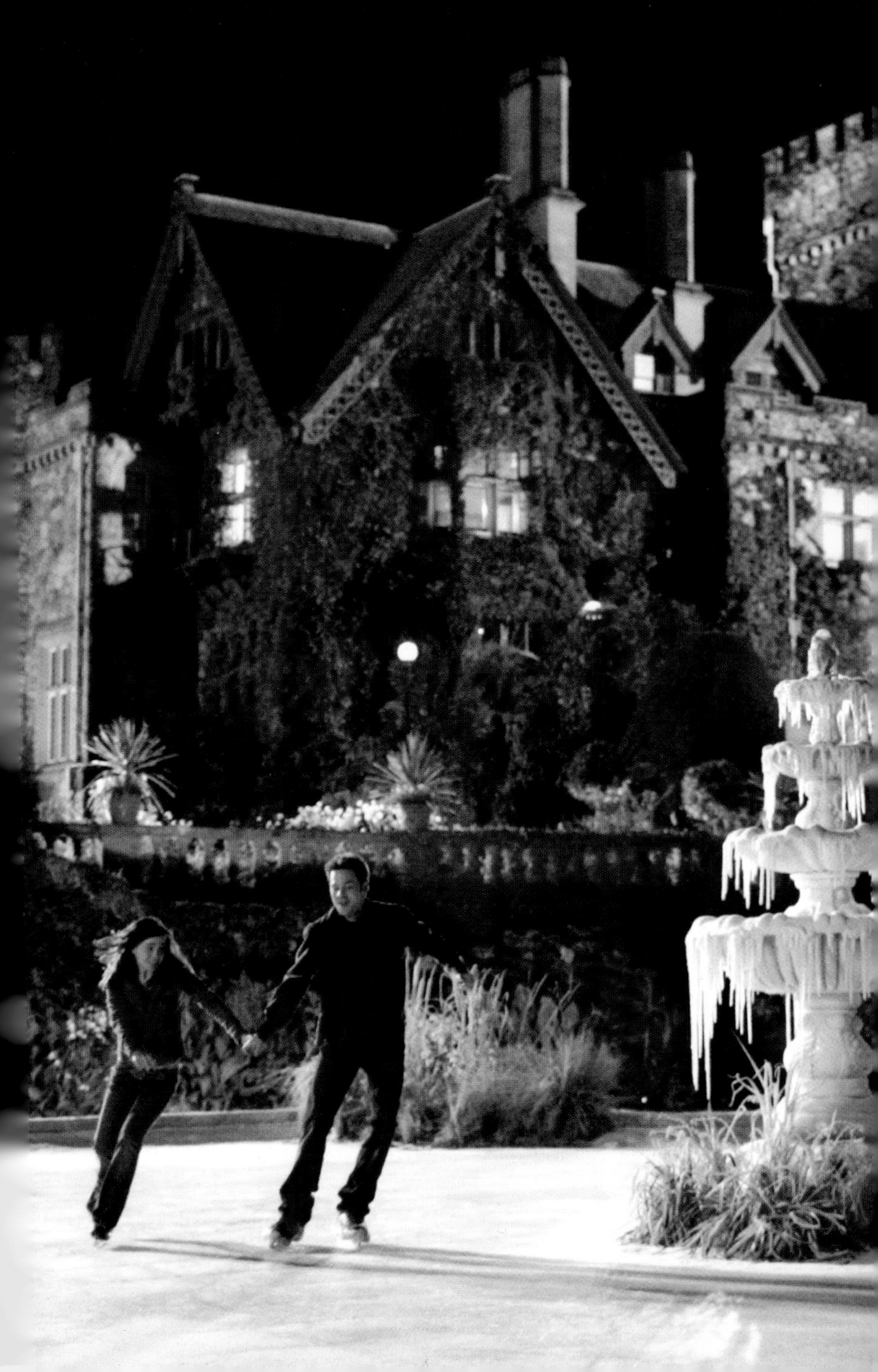

cars. The school wasn't a secret anymore—and now hundreds of parents were hurrying to enroll their mutant children in the best academy in the country.

Storm smiled at the sight. She was glad that the school would go on. It was a safe haven in an uncertain world. Not just for her, but for all mutants.